Travels Through The Underground Railroad

Akeira's Journey

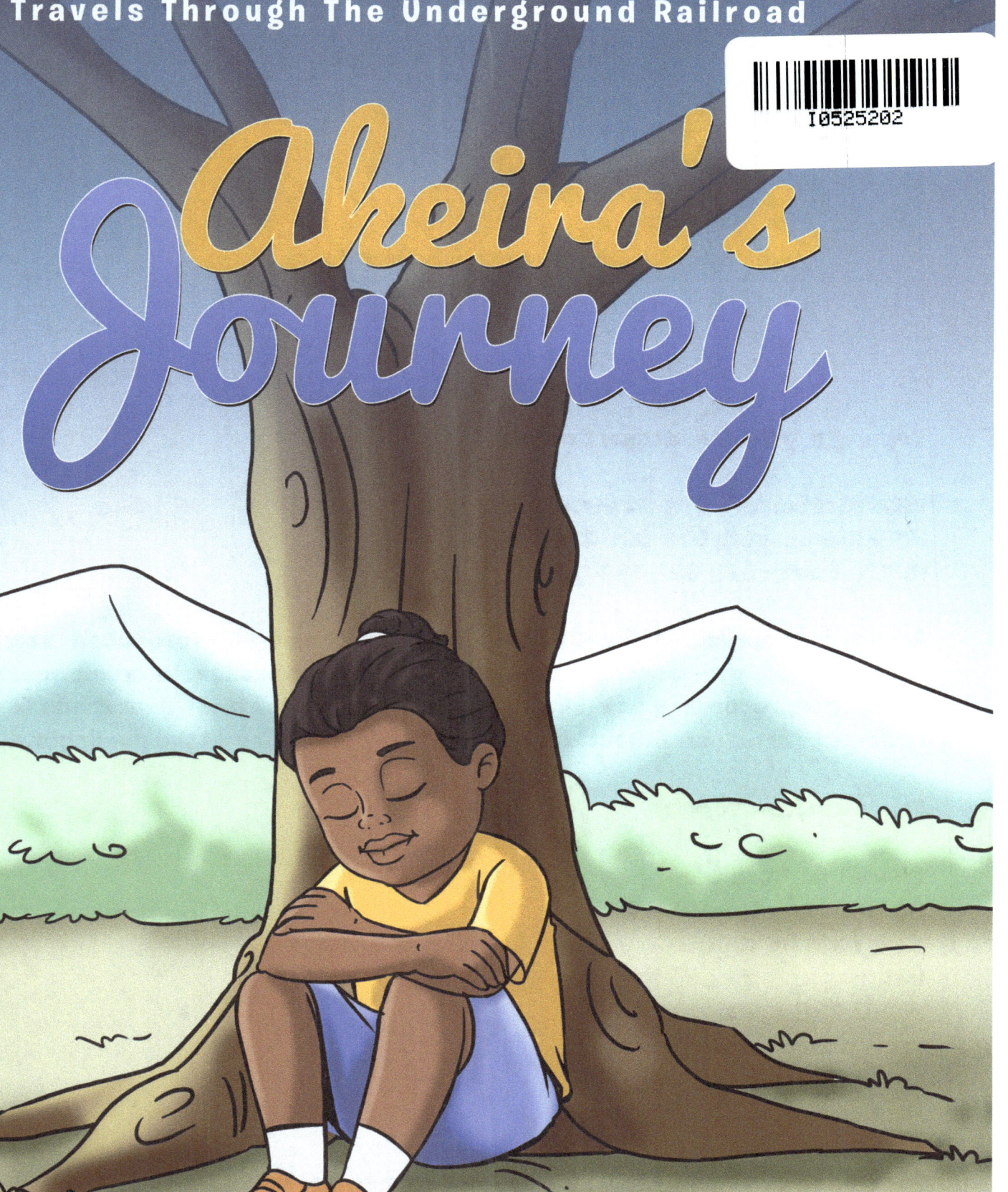

MATTHEW CRAMER

Copyright © 2018 Matthew Cramer

ISBN (Softcover): 978-621-959-019-8
ISBN (Hardcover): 978-621-434-000-2
ISBN (eBook): 978-621-434-001-9

Printed in New York by:

OMNIBOOK CO.
99 Wall Street, Suite 118
New York, NY 10005
USA
+1 202-738-1322
www.omnibookcompany.com

First Edition

For e-book purchase: Kindle on Amazon, Barnes and Noble
Book purchase: Amazon.com, Barnes & Noble, and www.omnibookcompany.com
Omnibook titles may be purchased in bulk for educational, business, fund-raising, or sales promotional use. For more information please e-mail info@omnibookcompany.com

Akeira's Journey

Once upon a time, there was a little girl named Akeira. Akeira liked to play in the woods. She would always go to her special place by the pond under an old sycamore tree. One day Akeira was sitting under the old tree and watching the waves ripple over the pond. She slowly began to fall asleep.

Akeira drifted off to sleep and when she awoke everything had changed. The pond was the same, but the trees and bushes were different. Even the tree she was leaning against had gotten smaller. Akeira became frightened and decided to head home. As she walked through the woods she heard a little boy talking to himself. She peaked through the bushes and a little boy was standing on an old tree stump yelling into the woods. Akeira approached the young boy and asked,

"What are you doing?" The boy replied, "My name is Freddie Douglass, and I'm giving a speech! Well... actually, my name is Frederick Bailey, but I'm going to use the name Frederick Douglass so the slave-catchers won't get me." Akeira laughed and asked, "How can you give a speech when nobody is there?"

Freddie smiled and answered, "I'm practicing for when I'm older. I'm a slave now, but someday I want to be free and teach others."

Akeira looked at the little boy strangely. "I've never known a slave before. How did you become a slave?" she asked. Freddie smiled at Akeira and replied, "My grand momma told me our ancestors came from Africa and were all made into slaves. When I was born, I became a slave too. I grew up in Easton, Maryland. I never knew my mother and father. My grandparents raised me. We work for a slave master who doesn't think of us as people. We are treated very badly and can't do anything without asking the slave owner.

We're not even allowed to read. I had to give other kids food in order to learn to read. I saw a book called The Columbian Orator that will teach me to become a great speaker so I can help others who wish to be free. I also wish to start a newspaper telling everyone that slavery is wrong! I'll call it The North Star!" Freddie became very angry and exclaimed, "It's not fair that we have to be slaves! Someday I'll fight for the freedom for all black people!"

Suddenly, they heard someone yell, "Who is that over there in the woods?" Freddie whispered to Akeira, "Those are the slave catchers. We must go now. If they catch us in the woods they'll hurt us!"

Akeira and Freddie ran away from the horrible men. She was shocked and very scared, and had no idea that people had gone through so much during slavery. Akeira ran as hard as she could in the direction she thought would lead her home. However, things didn't seem familiar. She stopped to catch her breath, and look for Freddie, but he was already gone. Lost in the woods, and scared of those awful slave catchers, she sat down on a rock and began to cry.

A tiny voice came out of the bush by the road, and asked Akeira, "Why are you crying?" The voice belonged to a little girl. Akeira whimpered, "I'm lost and scared of the horrible slave catchers!" The little girl introduced herself, "Hi, I'm Araminta, but you can call me Harriet. That's my momma's name...I like that better! I'll help you find your way home. I always see black people lost in these woods. One kid told me he was trying to go to the North to be free. I helped him by hiding him in my secret place where the slave catchers couldn't find him."

Akeira wiped her tears and said gratefully, "Thank you! I miss my family and want to go home." Harriet said in a determined voice, "Then that's what we're going to do! We're going to get you home and away from these bad people." Akeira's eyes lit up with hope as she asked, "What ever happened to the little boy?" Harriet replied, "He followed the Underground Railroad to freedom in the North. He followed the North Star all the way to Pennsylvania. When I'm old enough, I'm going to escape and be free too. I'm going to go to Pennsylvania and be a free woman. Then I'm going to free my sister, my brother, my momma and papa too. In fact, I'm going to try to save as many people as I can. Those ol' slave catchers won't ever catch me."

Akeira was very happy that Harriet would help her. She walked with Harriet along an old dirt road until they heard the sound of horses coming toward them. Harriet grabbed Akeira's hand, and together they ran and hid in the bushes. They peered through the leaves with frightened eyes, and saw two horses carting an old buggy passing right in front of them.

A poor-looking white man and woman stopped very close to where Harriet and Akeira were hiding. Harriet whispered to Akeira, "They won't hurt us. That's Mrs. Lucretia Mott and Mr. Mott. They're friends of the slaves. Although they're white people, they believe black people should not be slaves and treated badly."

Harriet led Akeira out of the bushes, as she called out to the people in the buggy, "Hi Mr. and Mrs. Mott!" The couple smiled and responded, "Hello Harriet! What are you doing in the woods, and who is your little friend?" Akeira looked at Harriet with an annoyed expression, and whispered, "I'm not little...I'm six!!" Harriet smiled at Akeira and replied to the couple, "This is Akeira and she's lost and wants to go home. Can you help her?" They shook their heads yes. Akeira described the pond where she fell asleep. The Motts allowed Akeira to hide in back of their buggy, and covered her in a large blanket before they rode off.

Akeira was very tired, and she nodded off to sleep. When the buggy stopped, she opened her eyes. As she rubbed the sleep from her eyes, she noticed that she was nowhere near the pond close to her home. However, she noticed a large river and there were huge ships everywhere. No one seemed to mind that she was alone. She looked up and saw a sign with the word "Pennsylvania" on it. The nice couple had taken her to the North to be free. The Motts dropped off Akeira and said goodbye. Akeira thanked the Motts, but was disappointed because she just wanted to go back home.

Akeira saw a little boy carrying things on and off a ship. She asked him, "Excuse me, where are we?" The boy stared at her with a puzzled look and said, "We're in Philadelphia!" Akeira smiled and said, "My daddy's from the Philadelphia area. I'm Akeira, and I'm from Maryland. Is everyone here free?" The little boy replied, "Most of the people here are free. You're in the North now. My name is Henry Garnet." Akeira asked, "How did you become free?" Henry told her how his parents had asked their slave owner if they could attend a funeral. Once they got permission to go, they ran off to the North. They moved away from Maryland to be free.

Henry started telling Akeira about his family. He was especially proud of his grandfather, and fondly described him to Akeira. "My grandpa was an African warrior prince." Henry said as his face lit up in admiration. "He was captured while trying to fight the slave catchers in Africa." He also told Akeira how his grandfather hated being a slave, and said that he would like to take many blacks back to Africa by ship.

Henry also told Akeira about his dreams of becoming a warrior like his grandfather someday. He told Akeira, "One day we'll be fighting for our freedom. I'm going to lead an army of black soldiers to fight for our right to be treated the same as white people. My grandfather fought the slave catchers so his family could be safe and free. I want to be just like him. When I grow up, I want to lead my people to their freedom so they won't have to be beaten and treated badly." Akeira nodded her head in agreement and said, "It's a horrible thing to be a slave. I hope you can do all of the things you talked about. All people should be treated the same no matter what their skin color is!"

By now, Akeira began wondering how she was going to get back to her home in Maryland. She didn't want to run into those mean slave catchers, but knew that her parents must be very worried about her now. She said goodbye to Henry, and started wandering around the city of Philadelphia.

As Akeira began walking down the old stone road, she looked up in awe at the old buildings. She wasn't watching her step, and suddenly she tripped over the foot of a little boy who was sitting on the steps of an old building. Akeira stumbled to the ground, and turned to the little boy. "Excuse me, I didn't see you there," she said, embarrassed. The little boy, who was writing in his book, looked up, giggled and said, "You should be more careful! Are you OK?" Akeira replied, "Yes, I'm fine. What are you writing?" The little boy answered, "I was just starting a journal of all the people I help." He reached for Akeira's hand and helped her up. "You can be the first person that I write about," he explained proudly. He then turned his attention back to the book and began writing.

The little boy introduced himself to Akeira. "My name is Willy Still. What is your name?" Akeira told the boy her name and asked him, "How do you plan on helping people?" Willy's eyes lit up. He responded, "I want to help all of the slaves in the South find their way to the North. I was born free, but a lot of kids aren't as lucky as me. Before I was born my parents were slaves in the South. They escaped from Maryland and lived as free people in New Jersey. They had to leave two of my brothers there. I've never met them. I hope someday they can find their way to the North and I'll help them to freedom." Akeira became sad when Willy spoke of his family. She asked Willy, "I'm from Maryland, but I wasn't a slave. How can I get back there?"

Willy thought for a second and then stood up. "You can follow the Underground Railroad! But I never heard of anyone wanting to go back to the South," he said, scratching his head. "I understand that you want to see your family. My momma and four of my brothers were captured from the North and taken back to the South. When she escaped again that's when she had to leave two of my brothers. I'll meet my brothers someday."

Willy grabbed Akeira's hand and said, "Let's go. I'll take you to someone that can help you get to the South." The walk was very long and they passed by several empty trolley cars. Akeira asked, "Why don't we take the trolleys instead of walking?" Willy responded, "It's a pretty long walk but we can't ride on the trolley cars. They don't allow black people on the cars. They don't want us to mix with white people. My feet hurt sometimes from walking so far, but they never let me on the trolley car. I'm going to ride on that trolley all day one of these days. I'm going to make sure it happens!" Akeira didn't mind walking. She was very happy to finally be heading back home.

After a very long walk, Willy and Akeira arrived at a man's house on the other side of Philadelphia. The man was Mr. Samuel D. Burris. Willy told Akeira, "Mr. Burris works for the Underground Railroad and he can help you get to your home in Maryland." Mr. Burris smiled at Akeira and said, "I'll help you, but why would you want to go down there? It's very dangerous to travel to the South!" Akeira looked up at the man and his bushy black beard and said, "I have to get back to my parents. I miss them very much!" Mr. Burris stroked his beard for a moment in deep thought. Although he didn't think it was a very good idea, he decided to help Akeira anyway.

Akeira said goodbye to Willy, and jumped in a horse carriage with Mr. Burris. They headed south, and started the long journey back to Maryland. During the long ride, Mr. Burris began talking about his other travels to the South. He told Akeira about the time he was captured in southern Delaware and sold into slavery, although he was born as a free man. He said to Akeira, "Even as a free man, if you help slaves to be free, the law says you can be sold into slavery. I decided long ago that I'd rather be sold into slavery, than watch my black brothers being treated like animals without helping them." Akeira asked the kind man, "How did you become free again after they sold you into slavery?" The man let out a very loud laugh, and bellowed, "Ha, ha, ha! A white friend from Philadelphia came down to Delaware and pretended to be southern slave buyer. He had never seen a slave being sold, and had to watch what everyone else was doing to bid on me. He rescued me and took me home." Akeira smiled and said, "I've learned during my time away from home that there were many white people that helped black people make it to freedom. Not all white folks are like those awful slave owners and slave catchers!" Mr. Burris smiled at Akeira and nodded his head in agreement.

When Mr. Burris got to the Maryland border that separated the North from the South, an older white gentleman was standing there in the road by a horse and carriage. By his side was a little boy that looked like Freddie. Mr. Burris told Akeira, "This is as far as I can take you. I promised myself never to go into the South again after almost being sold into slavery." Akeira looked over at the little boy and the man. It actually was Freddie! Akeira jumped from the wagon and ran toward Freddie in excitement. "Freddie! It's so great to see you," she yelled out with a big smile. Akeira was so happy, she gave Freddie a big hug. After hugging Freddie, her smile gave way to an expression of concern. She looked up and asked him, "Who is the man that you're with?" Freddie told her how he was caught when he and Akeira were running away from the slave catchers. The mean slave catchers were going to sell him in Dover, Delaware to another slave owner, when Mr. Garrett rescued him. Freddie then stated, "He's taking me back to my grandma and grandpa. I'm not ready to be free without my family, but someday I'll travel to the North!"

Akeira climbed into the carriage with Freddie and was taken back to the area where they first met. She looked around, and saw a small piece of the dress she was wearing. She knew it was the way back home. She quickly ran through the woods and came to the pond where she had fallen asleep. Her eyes lit up and filled with tears of joy as she ran to her favorite tree. She was so happy to be back to a place that looked familiar. She curled up under the old sycamore tree, but because she was tired from her long journey, she quickly fell asleep. As she drifted off to sleep, she had a dream of her big adventure, and of all the great people she met along the way.

When Akeira woke up everything had changed again. Everything looked like it did before. She looked around and started yelling for Freddie, but no one answered. She jumped up and ran through the woods. She ran so fast she didn't see someone working in the yard. She ran into the back of his legs. She looked up and saw her father smiling down on her. Akeira screamed, "DADDY!!!" Her father picked her up and gave her a big hug and a kiss. She told her father she missed him very much. Her father looked at her strangely and said to her, "I missed you too princess, but you've only been gone for an hour. Why do you look so shocked to see me?" Akeira told him of her wild journey and all of the people she met. She said to her father, "Daddy, I never want to be a slave!" Her father gave her another big hug and said, "Because of people like Frederick Douglass, Harriet Tubman, Henry Garnet, and many other special people, you will never ever have to be!"

Historical biographies

Frederick Douglass

Frederick Douglass (February 17, 1818 - February 20, 1895) was an American abolitionist, editor, orator, author, statesman and reformer. Called "The Sage of Anacostia" and "The Lion of Anacostia," Douglass was one of the most prominent figures of African American history during the 1800s, and one of the most influential lecturers and authors in American history. Douglass was a firm believer in the equality of all people, whether black, female, American Indian, or recent immigrant. He spent his entire life advocating the brotherhood of all humankind. One of his favorite quotations was: "I would unite with anybody to do right and with nobody to do wrong."

Frederick Augustus Washington Bailey, who later became known as Frederick Douglass, was born a slave in Talbot County, Maryland near Hillsboro. He was separated from his mother, Harriet Bailey, when he was still an infant

When Douglass was 12 years old, his master's wife, Sophia, broke the law by teaching him some letters of the alphabet. Thereafter, Douglass succeeded in learning to read from white children in the neighborhood in which he lived, and by observing the writings of the men with whom he worked.

In 1837, Douglass met Anna Murray, a free African-American, in Baltimore while he was still held in slavery. They were married soon after he obtained his freedom; Douglass escaped slavery on September 3, 1838, boarding a train to Havre de Grace, Maryland dressed in a sailor's uniform and carrying identification papers provided by a free black seaman. After crossing the Susquehanna River by ferry at Havre de Grace, Douglass continued by train to Wilmington, Delaware. From there Douglass went by steamboat to "Quaker City"– Philadelphia, Pennsylvania. His escape to freedom eventually led him to New York, the entire journey taking less than 24 hours.

Douglass later became the publisher of a series of newspapers: North Star, Frederick Douglass Weekly, Frederick Douglass' Paper, Douglass' Monthly and New National Era. The motto of The North Star was "Right is of no sex–Truth is of no color–God is the Father of us all, and we are all Brethren".

Douglass conferred with President Abraham Lincoln in 1863 on the treatment of black soldiers, and with President Andrew Johnson on the subject of black suffrage. His early collaborators were the white abolitionists. Douglass had five children; two of them, Charles and Rossetta, helped produce his newspapers.

By the time of the Civil War, Douglass was one of the most famous black men in the country, known for his oratories on the condition of the black race, and other issues such as women's rights.

In 1872, he became the first African American to receive a nomination for Vice President of the United States.

Frederick Douglass died in his adopted hometown of Washington D.C. He is buried in Mount Hope Cemetery in Rochester, New York

Harriet Tubman

Harriet Tubman (c. 1822-March 10, 1913), also known as "Moses of Her People," was an African-American abolitionist. An escaped slave, she made approximately 13 missions to rescue about 70 enslaved friends and family members to freedom in Canada using the Underground Railroad. During her lifetime she worked as a lumberjack, laundress, nurse, and cook. As an abolitionist, she helped liberate scores of slaves, and inspired many more to do so independently. During the Civil War she acted as intelligence gatherer, refugee organizer, raid leader, nurse, and fundraiser.

Born Araminta Ross in Dorchester County, Maryland, she was the fifth of nine children, four boys (Robert, Ben, Henry, and Moses) and five girls (Linah, Mariah Ritty, Soph, Araminta, and Rachel), of Ben and Harriet "Rit" Green Ross. When she was a young adult, she took the name Harriet, possibly in honor of her mother or due to a religious conversion. Around 1844, she married John Tubman, a free black man. When she ran away from Maryland, he chose not join her, but rather continued his free life in Dorchester County without her.

On September 17, 1849, Tubman and two of her brothers, Ben and Henry, ran away. Overcome with apprehension and fear, they returned two or three weeks later. Harriet, however, was determined to have her freedom, so soon thereafter she fled on her own, leaving behind husband. On the way to freedom in Philadelphia, she was assisted by members of the

Abolitionist movement, both black and white, who were instrumental in maintaining the regional branches of the Underground Railroad.

Called "Moses" by those she helped escape on the Underground Railroad, Tubman made many trips to Maryland to help family and friends escape. Tubman worked as a spy for the North during the American Civil War. Tubman was the first American woman to plan and lead a military operation, the raid at Combahee Ferry, in early June 1863. This raid freed over 750 slaves.

Tubman was successful in bringing away her parents and her four brothers – Ben, Robert, Henry, and Moses – but failed to rescue her sister Rachel, and Rachel's two children, Ben and Angerine.

In her later years, Harriet Tubman moved into a home aged African Americans that she had helped found. It was built on land which she had purchased, next to her own property in Auburn. She told stories of her adventures until her death on March 10, 1913. She was given a full military burial.

Lucretia Mott

Lucretia Coffin Mott (January 3, 1793 - November 11, 1880) was an American Quaker minister, abolitionist, social reformer and proponent of women's rights. She is credited as the first American "feminist" in the early 1800s but was, more accurately, the initiator of women's political advocacy.

Lucretia Coffin was born into a prominent Quaker family in Nantucket, Massachusetts.. At the age of thirteen she was sent to a boarding school run by the Society of Friends, where she eventually became a teacher. Her interest in women's rights began when she discovered that male teachers at the school were paid twice as much as the female staff. On 10 April 1811, Lucretia married James Mott, another teacher at the school. Ten years later, she became a Quaker minister.

Lucretia and her husband were both opposed to the slave trade and were active in the American Anti-Slavery Society. She moved to Philadelphia in 1821. She quickly became known for her persuasive speeches against slavery. Prior to her own involvement, many Quaker men had been involved in the abolitionist movement in the very early 1800s. Lucretia Mott was one of the first Quaker women to do advocacy work for abolition

Like many Hicksite Quakers including Hicks, Mott considered slavery an evil to be opposed. They refused to use cotton cloth, cane sugar, and other slavery-produced goods. She began to speak publicly for abolition, often traveling from her home in Philadelphia. Her sermons combined antislavery themes with broad calls for moral reform. Her husband supported her activism and they often sheltered runaway slaves in their home.

It should be noted that Quakers, when compared to other religious and social groups in America since its founding, were unusual in their equal treatment of women. They had a rich history and singular respect from the majority of American people of those times, mostly due to their advocacy and martyrdom for being conscientious objectors to war, and later their anti-slavery efforts.

Mott was successful in her abolitionist lobbying and punctuated her career with teaching the ropes of representative government's political advocacy to women coming up as women's and abolitionist advocates. In the 1830s she helped establish two anti-slavery groups.

In 1866 Mott joined with Stanton, Anthony, and Stone to establish the American Equal Rights Association. She was a leading voice in the Universal Peace Union, also founded in 1866. The following year, the organization became active in Kansas where Negro suffrage and woman suffrage were to be decided by popular vote.

She was posthumously inducted into the U.S. National Women's Hall of Fame.

Henry Highland Garnet

Henry Highland Garnet - (December 23, 1815 - February 13, 1882) was an African American abolitionist and orator. He was the first black minister to preach to the United States House of Representatives.

Garnet was born a slave near New Market in Kent County, Maryland. His grandfather was an African warrior prince, captured in combat, which might have been the source of Garnet's fiery spirit. Receiving permission to attend a funeral, he and his family instead escaped to free-state Pennsylvania in 1824. He spent two years at sea, as a cabin boy, cook, and steward. When he returned, he discovered that his family had split up due to threats of slave catchers. When Garnet was ten years old, the family reunited and moved to New York City, where from 1826 through 1833, Garnet attended the African Free School, and the Phoenix High School for Colored Youth. With several abolitionist friends, he established the Garrison Literary and Benevolent Association, but had to move the club because of racist feelings. Two years later, in 1835, he started to attend the Noyes Academy in Canaan, New Hampshire, but was driven away by an angry segregationist mob. The next year he injured his knee playing sports. It never recovered and his leg was amputated in 1840.

In 1842, he joined the American Anti-Slavery Society and frequently spoke at abolitionist conferences. One of his most famous speeches, "Call to Rebellion," was delivered August 1843 to the National Negro Convention in Buffalo, New York. The speech shared his views that slaves should act for themselves to achieve total emancipation. Garnet made references to some slave rebellions, stating that that could be a quick way for abolition if the slaves were brave enough. Frederick Douglass and William Lloyd Garrison, along with many other abolitionists, thought his ideas were too radical

By 1849 Garnet began to support emigration of blacks to Mexico, Liberia, or the West Indies, where they would have more opportunities. He also advocated establishing separate sections of the United States as black colonies. In 1850, he went to Great Britain on request of the Free Labor Movement, a group against slave-produced goods. He was popular, and spent two and a half years lecturing.

When the American Civil War erupted, his hopes for emigration dissolved. Instead, he turned his attention to the founding of black army units. In the New York draft riots of 1863, mobs were targeting blacks and black-owned buildings. Garnet was saved from death when his daughter quickly chopped their nameplate off their door before the mobs found them. When the authorization for black units came, Garnet helped with recruiting United States Colored Troops and then supported the black soldiers, preaching to many of them.

After the war, Garnet was appointed president of Avery College in Pittsburgh, Pennsylvania. He had always been sickly, but his health started to badly deteriorate in 1876. Garnet's last wish was to go to Liberia, live even just for a few weeks, and die there. His wish was granted and he became U.S. Minister to Liberia in late 1881, but died two months later. Garnet was given a state funeral by the Liberian government. Fredrick Douglass, who had not been on speaking terms with Garnet for many years, mourned his loss.

William Still

William Still (November 1819 or October 7, 1821 - July 14, 1902) was an African-American abolitionist, conductor on the Underground Railroad, writer, historian and civil rights activist.

The date of William Still's birth is given as October 7, 1821, by most sources, but he gave the date of November 1819 in the 1900 Census. He was born in Burlington County, New Jersey to Charity and Levin Still. Both his parents had come to New Jersey from the eastern shore of Maryland as ex-slaves. He was the youngest of eighteen siblings who moved to Philadelphia.

His father was the first of the family to move to New Jersey when he purchased his own freedom. Levin settled in Springtown near Medford and later Charity joined the family with their four children, when she escaped. Charity was recaptured and returned to slavery, but she escaped a second time and, with her two daughters, found her way to Burlington County, New Jersey, to join her husband. The two sons she left behind were sold to slaveowners in Alabama, in the deep South.

In 1844, William moved to Philadelphia, Pennsylvania, where, he began working as a clerk for the Pennsylvania Society for the Abolition of Slavery. When Philadelphia abolitionists organized a committee to aid runaway slaves reaching Philadelphia, Still became its chairman. By the 1850s, Still was a leader of Philadelphia's African-American community. In 1859 he attempted to desegregate the city's public transit system.

Often called "The Father of the Underground Railroad," Still helped as many as 60 slaves a month escape to freedom, interviewing each person and keeping careful records, including a brief biography and the destination of each person, along with any alias that they adopted, though he kept his records carefully hidden. During one interview of an escapee, it was discovered that the man, Peter Still, was his own brother. They had been separated since childhood, and his brother knew little about the rest of his family. Still later published The Underground Rail Road Records, which chronicles the stories and methods of some 649 slaves who escaped to freedom via the Underground Railroad. Peter Still later collaborated on a book detailing his experiences.

Samuel D. Burris

Samuel Burris (born 1808) was an African-American member of the Underground railway.

Burris was born in Willow Grove, then a small town in Delaware. Samuel was a free black man in a time when slavery was at its peak. Burris decided to move himself and his family to the safe city of Philadelphia, but from there he would make trips back and forth to the South to free other African Americans from slavery. Burris and his partner John Hunn started working with the underground railroad system in 1845. They worked closely together helping free slaves that were escaping from Delaware and Maryland.

Burris was well aware of what he was doing and the consequences that would apply to him if he were ever caught. In the state of Delaware helping slaves escape was as a very serious offence, and if caught the mandatory punishment was that one would be sold into slavery for a period of seven years. In June 1847 Burris was caught.

He was apprehended while helping a woman by the name of Marie Mathews escape from Dover, Delaware. Immediately after being captured Burris was put in the Dover jail for fourteen months while he awaited his trial. He was then convicted and automatically sentenced to be auctioned off into slavery. When Burris' friends who were active abolitionists found he was about to be sold they acted to free him. One of them posed as a slave buyer and bought Burris, then set him free.

The man who "purchased" Burris was Isaac Flint. Once Isaac had his friend back they left Delaware with no intentions to ever return there again.

Thomas Garrett

Thomas Garrett (August 21, 1789 - January 25, 1871) was an abolitionist and leader in the Underground Railroad movement before the American Civil War.

Garrett was born into a prosperous landowning Quaker family on their homestead called "Thornfield" in Delaware County, Pennsylvania. The house in which he lived until 1822, which was built around 1800, still stands today in Upper Darby Township.

In a family already inclined to abolitionism, Thomas was exceptionally dedicated. When a family Servent was kidnapped by men who planned to sell her as a slave in the South, he tracked them down and released her.

A follower of the schismatic Quaker leader Elias Hicks, Garrett split with his orthodox family and moved to Wilmington in the neighboring slave state of Delaware to strike out on his own and pursue his struggle against slavery. He established an iron mongering business and made it prosper.

All the while as he worked to dominate the iron trade in Wilmington, he secretly worked as a Station Master on the last stop of the Underground Railroad in the state. At his house in

Wilmington, fugitive slaves would stay in hidden chambers overnight before they made the final push into the free state of Pennsylvania. The authorities were aware of his activities and he was arrested more than once. During his trial in 1848 for assisting runaway slaves, he was told by the judge that the fine would be waived if Garrett promised to stop his illegal activities. Garrett took the opportunity to address the courtroom declaring "Friend, I haven't a dollar in the world, but if thee knows a fugitive who needs a breakfast, send him to me." The subsequent fines and penalties bankrupted him, but soon he again prospered. In 1860, the slave state of Maryland offered a $10,000 reward for information leading to his arrest and conviction for "stealing" slaves.

During the period before the Civil War, Garrett worked closely with William Lloyd Garrison and Harriet Tubman (who passed through his station many times). He estimated that before the war he assisted 2,246 fugitives and during the war an additional 73. During the war, his house was guarded by black volunteers.

At his funeral, Garrett's body was borne by freed blacks who declaimed him "Our Moses." A municipal park in Wilmington is named Tubman-Garrett Riverfront Park after the two Underground Railroad agents and friends.

9 786219 590198